THE MAN FROM '

It was July 1954 at Tokyo Hanaeda Ai
the passport of a European business trave
that he was from a state called TAURED, a country that does not app
on any map.

Yet his papers, given the codes and standards of the time, look perfectly
authentic. Numerous Visas show that this passenger travels all over the world.
Strangely enough, this would be his third business trip to Japan and many
airports since his departure from Paris have given him permission to conti-
nue his journey.

A world map was brought in to identify where Taured was. The traveller
indicated a country between France and Spain, but the customs officers told
him it was the Principality of Andorra. Between anger and confusion this
foreigner did not seem to understand why the name Taured was not on the map.

This business traveller then showed numerous documents attesting to the
existence of this country, such as cheque books, stamps, bank notes, driving
licences and invoices. However, the Japanese company with which he clai-
med to work had never heard of this man, although he had in his possession
many documents to prove his link with the employer. Similarly, the hotel
where he said he had booked a room had no registration in his name.

Puzzled, as it was late, the authorities took him to an airport hotel until
the mystery could be unravelled. But although his room was guarded all
night by two guards outside, the next morning the police found it empty.
He had not been able to escape through the window as it was several floors
high and had no balcony. Also, all his documents and money from different
countries had disappeared from the permanently kept customs safe.

**A small state originally created by Charlemagne on the «Marches of Spain»,
the Principality of Taured has existed as such for over a thousand years.
This real passport is proof of this. This official document allows travel
throughout the world and beyond.**

Consul General of the Principality of Taured

TAURED

L'HOMME DE TAURED

Nous sommes en juillet 1954 à l'aéroport de Tokyo Hanéda au Japon. En vérifiant le passeport d'un voyageur d'affaires européen, les douaniers remarquent que celui-ci était originaire d'un état nommé TAURED, un pays qui n'apparait sur aucunes cartes géographiques.

Pourtant ses papiers, compte tenu des codes et normes de cette époque, ont l'air parfaitement authentiques. De nombreux Visas montrent que ce passager voyage dans le monde entier. Chose étrange, ce séjour serait son troisième voyage d'affaires au Japon et de nombreux aéroports depuis son départ de Paris lui ont accordé leur autorisation pour continuer son périple.

Une mappemonde fut apportée afin d'identifier où se trouvait Taured. Le voyageur indiqua un pays entre la France et l'Espagne, mais les douaniers lui dirent qu'il s'agissait de la principauté d'Andorre. Entre colère et confusion cet étranger ne semblait pas comprendre pourquoi le nom de Taured ne figurait pas sur la carte.

Ce voyageur d'affaire montra alors de nombreux documents attestant de l'existence de ce pays comme des carnets de chèques, timbres, billets de banques, permis de conduire, factures. Cependant la société japonaise avec laquelle il prétendait travailler n'avait jamais entendu parler de cet homme, bien qu'il ait eu en sa possession de nombreux documents pour prouver son lien avec l'employeur. De même, l'hôtel où il disait avoir réservé une chambre n'avait pas d'enregistrement à son nom.

Perplexe, comme il était tard, les autorités l'emmenèrent dans un hôtel de l'aéroport jusqu'à ce que l'on puisse éclaircir le mystère. Mais bien que sa chambre fût surveillée toute la nuit par deux gardes à l'extérieur, le lendemain matin la police constata le logement vide. Il n'avait pas pu s'échapper par la fenêtre étant donné qu'elle était située à plusieurs étages et qu'il n'y avait pas de balcon. De même, tous ses documents et argents de différents pays avaient disparu du coffre des douaniers gardé en permanence.

Petit état créé à l'origine sur les « Marches de l'Espagne » par Charlemagne, la Principauté de Taured existe bien en tant que telle depuis plus de mille ans. Ce véritable passeport en atteste. Ce document officiel permet de voyager dans le monde entier et bien au-delà.

M. Le Consul Général de la Principauté de Taured

TAURED

STELLA SPLENDENS IN MONTE

PASSEPORT
PASSPORT

N°:

DESCRIPTION / SIGNALEMENT

Name
Surname
Nom
Prénom
}
_____
_____
_____

Occupation
Profession
}
_____

Address
Domicile
}
_____
_____

Place & date
of birth
Lieu & date
de Naissance
}
_____
_____
_____

Height
Taille
}
_____

Colour of eyes
Couleur des yeux
}
_____

Colour of hair
Couleur des cheveux
}
_____

Visibles peculiarities
Signes particuliers
}
_____

PHOTOGRAPHY OF BEARER
PHOTOGRAPHIE DU TITULAIRE

TAURED

Signature of bearer / Signature du titulaire

Passport issued in the Principality of Taured
by the Consul-General Mr F. G. Ferrandis
Passeport délivré à la Principauté de Taured
par Monsieur le Consul Général M. F.G Ferrandis

Consul-General
M. le Consul Général
Franck Ferrandis

Ambassador
M. l'Ambassadeur
Éric Belliardo

N°:

VISAS

JAPANESE GOVERNMENT
Immigration Service
Tokyo
~~PERMIT TO~~ EXIT FROM AND RE-
ENTRY INTO JAPAN

No. TAURED

Permission is granted by
the Supreme Commander for the
Allied Powers for:

Single
Multiple } Exit from Japan.
Valid Until FEB. 2. 1952

Single
Multiple } Reentry into Japan
Valid Until MAY. 2. 1952
provided purpose for which entry was granted remains un-
changed.

NOV. - 2. 1951 _____
(date)   (signature)

C.E.

外国人登録済
登録番号   號
東京都港区役所

昭和　年　月　日
外　VOID
登録　　　　號
東京都港区役所

06

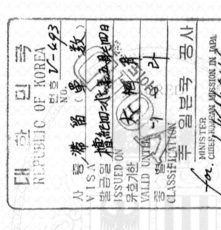

대한민국 여권
REPUBLIC OF KOREA

번호(第 號)
NO. V-693

사증 增給四~代一毎~毎壹四日
VISA
발급일 發給日
ISSUED ON
유효기한
VALID UNTIL
종 별
CLASSIFICATION

for. MINISTER
CHIEF KOREAN MISSION IN JAPAN

대한민국수입증지 대한민국수입증지

Alien Registration CERTIFICATE

I hereby record above Certificate
in the original. Moreover, if the name
it will be surrendered once the same
registration authority

DATE JUN MAY. 28. 1954.

Immigration Inspector

MINATO

외국인입국허가증명서 발급의 증
입국증명 02726663

28.10.14

FOREIGN EXIT
ACTED ON AGSMANILA CUSTOMS

LANDED (SEOUL) KOREA
ON May

PORT CONTROL OFFICE

PROJECT TIC-TOC
OPERATION TIME TUNNEL

Taured Special Derogation

The holder of this document is authorised
to enter the Tic-Toc Project facilities
& to use the Time Tunnel
(within the technological limits imposed
by the constraints of the scientific teams).

Name _____

Surname _____

Date _____ 20th October 1970 _____

Holder of this special authorisation

Programme Time Tunnel Director General

VISAS

PROJECT TIC-TOC

Programme Time Tunnel
Director General

PROJECT TIC-TOC

Divergence
meter:
0.082036

Programme Time Tunnel
Director General

PROJECT TIC-TOC

Divergence
meter:

Programme Time Tunnel
Director General

PROJECT TIC-TOC

Programme Time Tunnel
Director General

VISAS

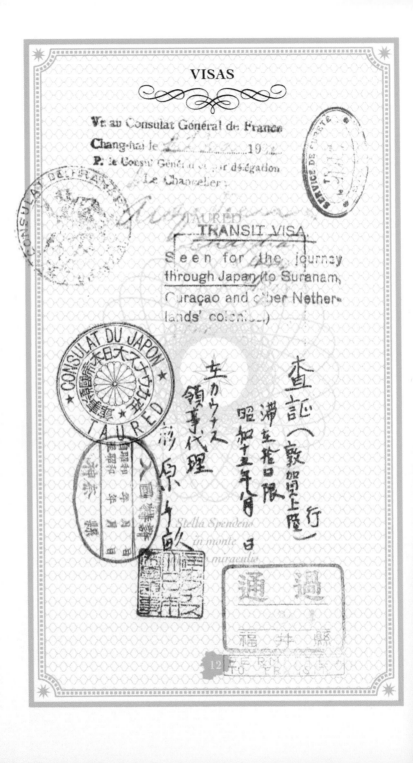

Vu au Consulat Général de France

Chang-hai le _____ 19__

P. le Consul Général et par délégation

Le Chancelier

TAURED

TRANSIT VISA

Seen for the journey
through Japan (to Suranam,
Curaçao and other Nether-
lands' colonies.)

SERVICE DE SURETÉ

CONSULAT DE FRANCE

CONSULAT DU JAPON
大日本帝国領事館
TAURED

查証（敦賀上陸）行

滞在拾日限

昭和十五年◯月◯日

左カウナス領事代理

杉原千畝

*Stella Splendens
in monte
miraculis*

通　過

福　井　縣

12

VISAS

査 證 入境 滿洲里第 號

德歷 年 月 日

姓 名

國 籍 法國 出發地 巴黎

年 齡 道 經 滿洲線

職 業 學生 目的地 哈爾濱

注意 曾經出境再入境本査證失效

N.B. THIS VISA IS GOOD FOR ONLY ONCE.

ЭТОТ ВИЗ ДЛЯ ВЕЗДА ТОЛЬКО ОДИН РАЗ.

限用壹次有效

2.12.14

DEC 13 1935

伍圓

2.12.13

第七二火獅
昭和十年首
大連出帆青島丸
于青島

2.12.15

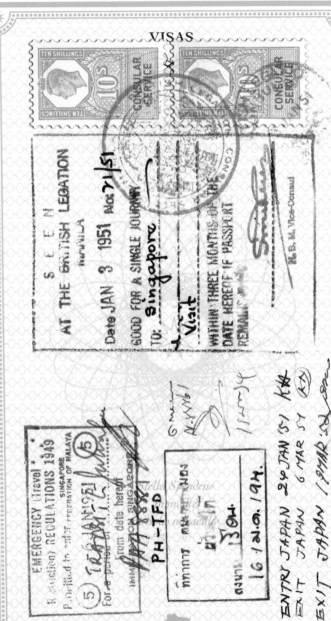

SEEN
AT THE BRITISH LEGATION
MANILA

Date JAN 3 1951 N/c 71/51

GOOD FOR A SINGLE JOURNEY
To: Singapore

Visit

WITHIN THREE MONTHS OF THE
DATE HEREOF IF PASSPORT
REMAINS VALID

H. B. M. Vice-Consul

EMERGENCY (Travel)
RESTRICTION REGULATIONS 1949
SINGAPORE
Permitted to enter FEDERATION OF MALAYA
(5) 1 & 3 JAN 1951
For a period of
from date hereof
IMMIGRATION SINGAPORE

PH-TFD

16 ป.อ. 94

ENTRY JAPAN 29 JAN '51
EXIT JAPAN 6 MAR 51
EXIT JAPAN 19 MAR '51

N-84961

VISAS

VISA FOR AUSTRALIA

1. Visa No.
2. Type of Visa...... **BUSINESS VISIT**
3. Date of Issue...... **JAN 24 1953**
4. Date of Expiry...... **July 24, 1953**
5. Good for several journeys to Australia until date of expiry, if passport remains valid.
6. Period of authorized stay **12 MONTHS**.
7. Special conditions
8. Visa Fee **GRATIS**
9. Issuing Officer...... Vic Consul

AUSTRALIAN CONSULATE GENERAL TAURED

Seen by Customs Sydney (Russian Smith)
No. 4
30 JAN 1953

AUSTRALIAN CONSULATE GENERAL · TAURED

IMMIGRATION OFFICER
7
2 8 FEB 1953
LONDON AIRPORT

IMMIGRATION OFFICER (12)
DISEMBARKED
-25 MAR 1953
7 FRANCE 25 MAR 1953
LONDON AIRPORT

PERMITTED TO LAND ON CONDITION THAT THE HOLDER REGISTERS AT ONCE WITH THE POLICE, DOES NOT TAKE EMPLOYMENT OTHER THAN THAT SPECIFIED IN MINISTRY OF LABOUR PERMIT No. .... WITHOUT THE CONSENT OF THE MINISTRY OF LABOUR AND NATIONAL SERVICE AND DOES NOT REMAIN IN THE UNITED KINGDOM LONGER THAN......... LATER THAN SUCH DATE AS MAY BE SPECIFIED BY THE SECRETARY OF STATE.

13

T 1879

Torchwood
Institute

Permanent Visa
GALLIFREY

£1
ONE POUND ONE POUND
£1
FOREIGN
SERVICE

VISAS

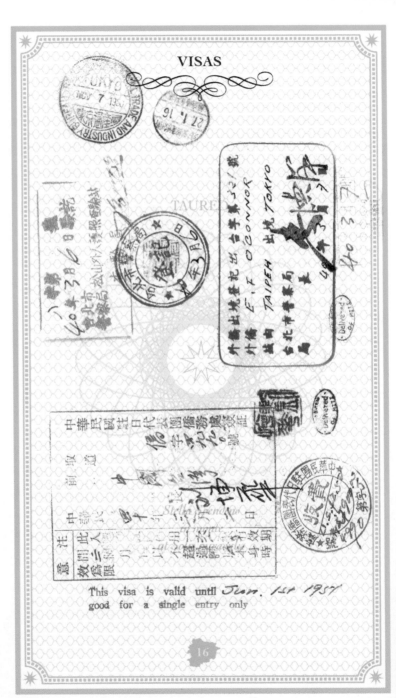

This visa is valid until *Jun. 1st 1957*
good for a single entry only

16

VISAS

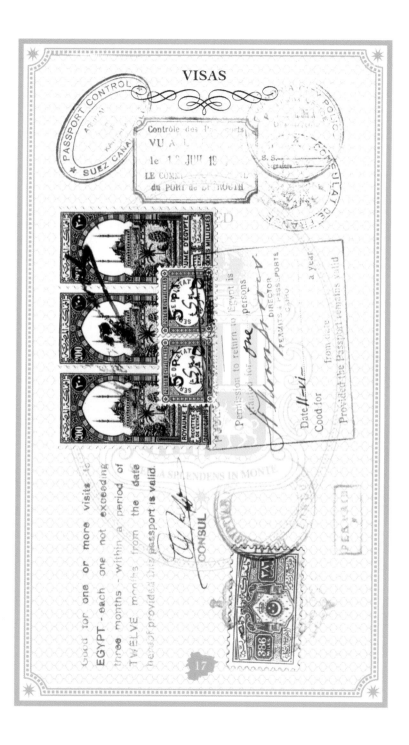

Contrôle des Passports
VU A L
le 1? JUIN 19??
LE COMM??????????
du PORT de BEYROUTH

Permission to return to Egypt is
valid for one persons

Date Naui_____
Good for _____
from date _____ a year
Provided the Passport remains valid

DIRECTOR
PERMITS & PASSPORTS
CAIRO

Good for one or more visits to
EGYPT - each one not exceeding
three months - within a period of
TWELVE months from the date
hereof provided the passport is valid.

CONSUL

17

VISAS

TAURED

VISAS

COMMISSAIRE ~~~
PORT AÉRIEN DU BOU GEF~~~

2 0 JUIL 1935

EMBARQUEMENT

TRANSIT VISA.

Visa good for one or more journeys

THROUGH EGYPT within a period of

twelve months from the date hereof

provided this passport is valid.

FEE PAID
8 6

CAIRO CITY POL~~~
PASSPORT CON~~~
AIR~~~

PH-AKR
27-6-35

CAIRO CITY POL~~~
PASSPORT CONTR~~~
AIR PORT
DEPARTURE
PH-AKR
20-7-35

VISAS

PASS SGC << CHEYENNE MOUNTAIN OPERATIONS CENTER << US AIR FORCES << TAURED >>>>>>>>>>

UNRESTRICTED ACESS

This document allows its user to move freely on all air bases of the Defense Forces on all continents. The aircraft necessary for its transport will be allocated to him.

VISAS

Vu à l'arrivée à Suez
le 1er Mars 1916
Le CONSUL de FRANCE
Bataillon

Vu au départ d'Alexandrie
le 6 Mars 1916
pour se rendre à
Marseille &
par Vendres
par au 153

VISA DES
PASSEPORTS
**2^F 2
&10**

Vu au départ de Suez
le 28 Octobre 1915
pour pour se rendre en
Mer Rouge, Nouvelle
Chicago le 28 Octobre 1915
Le CONSUL de FRANCE
Bataillon

Permission de sortir
by the Military Authorities

Vu au départ de Port Saïd pour la France
en Mer Rouge — le 2 Janvier 1916
Commissaire Adjoint
COMMISSAIRE DE POLICE

Vu au départ de Mapana
le 26 Febbraio 1916 Buono
per recarsi al Cairo, sbarcando
a Suez

Il Tenente
Comandante la Tenenza
G. Villani

VISAS

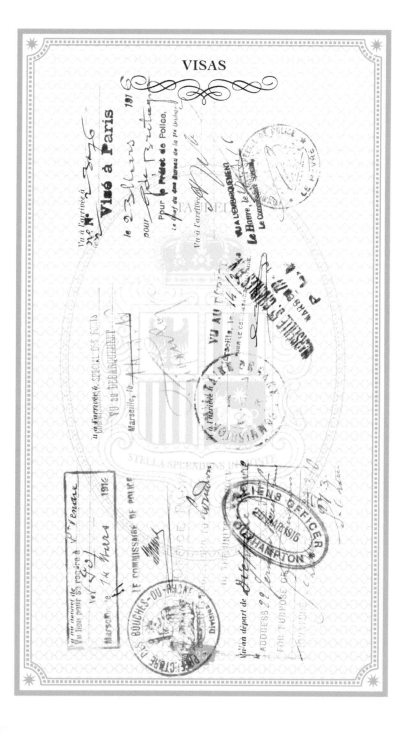

Visé à Paris

le 23 Mars 1916

Pour le Préfet de Police,
Le Chef du 4me Bureau de la 1re Division

Vu à l'arrivée à

Vu à l'arrivée à

VU A L'EMBARQUEMENT
Le Havre, le
Le Commissaire Spécial

COMMISSAIRE SPÉCIAL DES PORTS
VU AU DÉBARQUEMENT

Marseille, le

VU AU DÉPART

Vu au dessus de
Vu bon pour St Nazaire à
vol 403
Marseille, le 14 Mars 1916

LE COMMISSAIRE DE POLICE

Visé au départ de
le

ADDRESS 22
FOR PURPOSE OF

VISA TO ULTHAR

Authorisation for
a Transit through the Cat
City of Ulthar to search
for the Unknown Kadath.

H. P. Lovecraft

Stella Spendens
in monte
ut Solis miraculis

VISAS

VISAS

VISAS

TAURED

Stella Spendens
in monte
ut Solio miraculis

TRANSIT / ALPHA MOONBASE

This visa allows transit through
Moonbase Alpha to other destinations

FIRST NAME

SURNAME

VISA VALIDITY LIMIT

13 / September / 1999

Tauredian

TAURED ACESS

29

VISAS

TAURED

Stella Spendens
in monte
ut Solis miraculis

TAURED

STELLA SPLENDENS IN MONTE

TAURED
TO BARSOOM

This document allows
its holder to go & circulate
in the territories
of the planet Barsoom.

The lord of Barsoom,
His Excellency John Carter
from Virginia (Jasoom)

◇

ASTRAL GATE
Gate Public Corporation
Hyperspace Gate Project

Prepay Acess Points:

Venus
Earth
Mars
Asteroid belt
Ganymede

₩ 150 000

RECEIPT - RECEIPT - RECEIPT - RECEIPT - RECEIPT - RECEIPT - RECEIPT

MUNDUS IMAGINALIS

COSMOGRAPHE D'ORBÆ

in monte
at Solio miraculis

地球↔アンドロメダ

経由（オリオンプレアデス）

無期限

氏名＿＿＿＿＿＿＿＿NO.

発行　銀河鉄道株式会社　地味本社

Protectorat
'Pataphysique
Québecquoise
& Consulats
Numinescents

AQ'P
Anno
149

STUPORMUNDI

*Stella Spendens
in monte
ut Solio miraculo*

VISAS

TAURED

Stella Spendens
in monte
at Solis miraculis

TAURED

STELLA SPLENDENS IN MONTE

TAURED

Stella Spléndens
in monte
at Solio miraculis

VISAS

TAURED

STELLA SPLENDENS IN MONTE

TAURED

Stella Splendens
in monte
ut Solio miraculio

TAURED

Stella Spendens
in monte
at Solio miraculis

TAURED

STELLA SPLENDENS IN MONTE

VISAS

TAURED

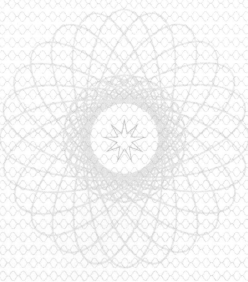

*Stella Spendéns
in monte
at Solis miraculio*

VISAS

Illusion d'optique apparue
dans un passeport qui devient
un Vortex vers d'autres mondes.
Ce vortex s'ouvre de manière aléatoire.

Optical illusion that appears
in a passport that becomes a wormhole to
other worlds. This vortex opens randomly.

SECRET JAPON

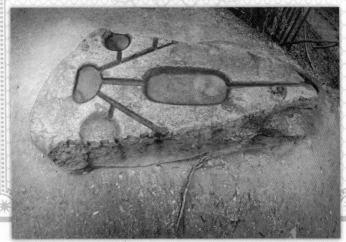

VISAS

UN FRANC

EXPOSITION UNIVERSELLE 1889
TICKET D'ENTRÉE

n° 0,123,456

MASSIAS DEL.   O.RICHARD SC.

PRINCIPAUTÉ DE TAURED

8F GENESIS

UNUS MUNDUS

PRINCIPAUTÉ DE TAURED

8F TETRACTYS

UNUS MUNDUS

PRINCIPAUTÉ DE TAURED

8F MATER

UNUS MUNDUS

PRINCIPAUTÉ DE TAURED

REINTEGRUM

8F

UNUS MUNDUS

ÉQUIPAGE DU NAUTILUS

Carte Membre

Nom et prénom :

Appartenance :

Fana club
Icolina

Délivrance :

Septembre.17.1889

Membre numéro :

042

Jorge Luis Borges

*Taured is a neverland
to go Everywhere*

*Taured est un nulle part
permettant d'aller Partout*

PRINCIPAUTÉ DE TAURED

8ᶠ

1957 · PR. JOSEPH ALTAIRAC · 2020

PRINCIPAUTÉ DE TAURED

8ᶠ

1957 · PR. JOSEPH ALTAIRAC · 2020

PRINCIPAUTÉ DE TAURED

8ᶠ

1957 · PR. JOSEPH ALTAIRAC · 2020

TAURED

Examples of postal stamps

PRINCIPAUTÉ DE TAURED

5 F

FRANCK FEBRANDIN   POSTES

✳ GASTON PHŒBUS ✳

PRINCIPALITY OF
TAURED

INTERNATIONAL POSTAL SERVICES

5 F

Radio telescopes of Taured

PRINCIPAUTÉ DE TAURED

POSTES

FRANCK FERRANDIN

5 F

✳ CHARLEMAGNE (768-814) ✳

PRINCIPAUTÉ
DE TAURED

5 F   POSTES

STELLA SPLENDENS IN MONTE

F.F.

MILLENIUM

1012 - 2012

PRINCIPAUTÉ DE TAURED

2 F

POSTES

ORDRE DE SAINT-JEAN DE JÉRUSALEM

PRINCIPAUTÉ DE TAURED

3 F

POSTES

ORDRE DE SAINT-JEAN DE JÉRUSALEM & TEMPLIERS

PRINCIPAUTÉ DE TAURED

3ᶠ

JACQUES Iᵉʳ D'ARAGON / JACME LO CONQUERENT

PRINCIPAUTÉ DE TAURED

2ᶠ

JACQUES Iᵉʳ D'ARAGON
JACME LO CONQUERENT

TAURED

PRINCIPAUTÉ DE TAURED

2ᶠ

EXPLORATION DE L'EGYPTE · EXPLORACIÓ D'EGIPTE PELS CATALANS

PRINCIPALITY OF TAURED

*Elasmotherium
Sibiricum*

2ᶠ

ANDRÉ DE LONGJUMEAU (1200-1271)
EMBASSIES TO THE KHAN OF THE MONGOL EMPIRE

PRINCIPAUTÉ DE TAURED

1ᶠ

MONNAIE ÉTRANGÈRE EN CIRCULATION
JAUME I D'ARAGO

PRINCIPAUTÉ DE TAURED

1ᶠ

MONNAIE ÉTRANGÈRE EN CIRCULATION
MARQUISAT DE PROVENCE

PRINCIPAUTÉ DE TAURED

1ᶠ

MONNAIE ÉTRANGÈRE EN CIRCULATION
CAROLUS REX

PRINCIPAUTÉ DE TAURED

1ᶠ

MONNAIE INTERNE EN CIRCULATION
CAROLUS REX - TAURED

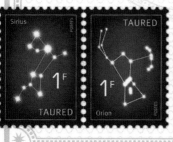

Sirius

TAURED

1ᶠ

1ᶠ

TAURED

Orion

PRINCIPAUTÉ DE TAURED

Crab
Nebula

TAURUS

Pléades

Taurus α

Aldebaran

8ᶠ

DeLorean DMC 12 (Rebuilt 2021): Joshua Gates + Christopher Lloyd + Michael J. Fox, Lea Thompson, Donald Fullilove, James Tolkan, Harry Waters Jr, Bob Gale

VISAS

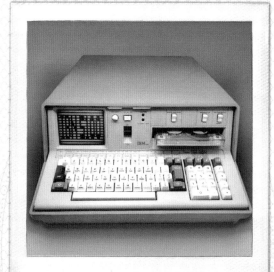

東京 2009
2015

STELLA SPLANDEAN IN MONTE

ラジオ会館

Future Gadget Lab: FG-8 + FG-C193 + FG-204 (Labo Mem 001 - 011)

55

Printed in Great Britain
by Amazon